בס"ד
לד' הארץ ומלואה

This book belongs to:

Please read it to me!

Dollars and Sense

For Janet and Kristen - G.Z.

First Edition – 2012 / 5772
Copyright © 2012 by HACHAI PUBLISHING
ALL RIGHTS RESERVED

Editor: D.L. Rosenfeld
Managing Editor: Yossi Leverton
Layout: Moshe Cohen

ISBN: 978-1929628-65-0
LCCN: 2012932833

HACHAI PUBLISHING
Brooklyn, New York
Tel: 718-633-0100 Fax: 718-633-0103
www.hachai.com   info@hachai.com

Printed in China

Glossary

Ima...............Mother
Mitzvah.........Commandment, good deed
Rebbi............Teacher
Shehakol........Blessing on certain foods, drinks
Tzedakah.......Charity

DOLLAR$
AND $ENSE

written by Tehilla Deutsch
illustrated by Glenn Zimmer

Hachai
PUBLISHING

Mrs. Markowitz waved
   as I rode up the street,
So I slowed down my bike,
   and I jumped to my feet.

She said, "Thanks to you, my house looks its best!
I was gone for a week, but who would have guessed?
You followed instructions, each one without fail,
You watered my plants, and you brought in the mail.

"You fed my fish daily – he looks so content,
And so, Eli Katz, you have earned every cent.
Take these five dollars; don't try to refuse."
"Well, thank you!" I grinned, looking down at my shoes.

She smiled at me, looking me right in the eye,
And said, "There is so much that money can buy,
So many nice things, but if you are clever,
You'll find the best kind that can last you forever."

I nodded my head, but I didn't think twice,
I was way too excited to hear her advice.
I happily bounced off to school with my stash,
Thinking of ways
I could spend all that cash.

Recess finally came! We played tag and we raced –
Until, out of breath and tomato-red faced,
I made a Shehakol and sipped my cold tea,
And that feeling I felt seemed the best there could be!

But later I lay in my bed, and I thought,
"What do I have left from the drink that I bought?
Next time I spend money, I'll learn from the past,
And spend it on something I'm certain will last."

The next afternoon, I made a quick stop,

On my way home from school, at the grocery shop.

Right there at the front of the store where you pay,

I saw chocolate and candy and gum on display.

"A whole pack of gum, THAT would last quite a while,"

I said to myself, as I reached for the pile.

I handed the cashier a one dollar bill,

Another one down, but I had three more still!

The gum was so soft and so perfectly sweet,
I trotted home happily,
chewing my treat.

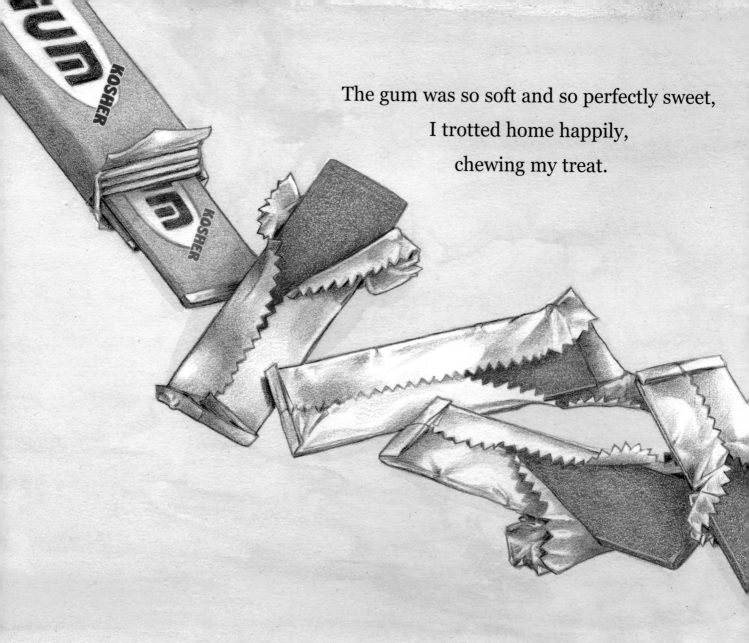

But just two days later, the pack had no more,
I had chewed the last piece, and my jaws were all sore.

A drink or a snack doesn't last, that was clear.
So what can I buy that will not disappear?

I know – a new toy – or a new game to play,
That's something I'll have with me day after day!

So I went to the toy store to find something fun,
There were all kinds of toys, but I had to pick one!

Then I spotted the yo-yos, the latest design,
"ON SALE FOR TWO DOLLARS," it said on the sign.

What a great buy! And these looked really nice,
I said to myself, "This is well worth the price!"

Well, using my yo-yo was fun, as I'd guessed,
I learned lots of tricks, and my friends were impressed.
But soon I got bored, and to my great dismay,
The string got all knotted and started to fray.

So this wasn't the answer. I let out a sigh,
Isn't there anything worthwhile to buy?
I had only one dollar bill to my name,
And nothing to show for the rest, what a shame!

"No more icy cold tea, no more sweet fruity gum,
Just an old, broken yo-yo," I thought, feeling glum.

I had to keep searching;
I had to be clever,
And find that one thing
that could last me forever.

"Eli," called Ima,
"Come here, won't you please?
I'm all out of cereal,
Yogurt, and cheese.

"Would you do me a favor
And run to the store?"
She gave me some cash,
And I dashed out the door.

I found what I needed and stood in the line,
When I noticed my neighbor, Yehuda Tzvi Fine.
Something was wrong; I could tell right away,
I decided to ask him if he was okay.

"Well, I was 'til a minute ago," he replied,
"But I've got a problem," the little boy sighed.
"I came here to buy some fresh bread for my mother,
But I lost a dollar, somehow or another.

"My very first time by myself at the store –
I guess I won't ever be sent anymore.
I wanted to show them that I'm not too small,
And losing that dollar won't help me at all."

While he stood there unhappily shaking his head,
I thought about what Mrs. Markowitz said.
Could this be my chance? My chance to be clever?
My chance to have something to last me forever?

I wanted to help him. I heard myself say,

"Yehudah Tzvi Fine, this must be your day!"

Then I gave him my dollar, my very last one,

And he grinned like a kid who just hit a home run!

So now, here I am, not a penny remaining,
But you can believe me that I'm not complaining.

When I think of his smile, that look on his face,
I know I have something I'd never replace.

A mitzvah like that,
It will not go away,
Or break, or get used up,
Or tangle or fray.

You'll find a chance too,

If you look and you try.

There's just nothing better

That money can buy!